D0452694

igloobooks

Published in 2014
by Igloo Books Ltd
Cottage Farm
Sywell
NN6 0BJ
www.igloobooks.com

Copyright © 2013 Igloo Books Ltd

All rights reserved. No part of this publication may be reproduced or transmitted in any form or by any means, electronic, or mechanical, including photocopying, recording, or by any information storage and retrieval system, without permission in writing from the publisher.
The measurements used are approximate.

HUN001 0514
2 4 6 8 10 9 7 5 3
ISBN 978-1-78197-627-2

Illustrated by Doreen Marts
Written by Melanie Joyce

Printed and manufactured in China

The Not-So
Perfect
Princess
igloobooks

Princess Pansy was very spoiled and liked to make lots of noise.

"I want more dresses!" she would cry. "I want books and games and toys!"

When Prince Cedric came to play,
Pansy pushed him onto the floor.

Then, Princess Tara visited and
they had a tug of war.

"You must learn to share," said the queen,
but Pansy just gave a frown.
She saddled up her pony, Neddy and
trotted into town.

Outside the little toyshop, excited children stood in line.
"We're queuing for the latest game," they said, pointing at the sign.
The game was nearly sold out. There was only one left in-store.

"I want it,"
whispered Pansy, because
she always wanted more.

Princess Pansy gave
a smile. She knew
exactly what to do.

"Gee up, Neddy.
Out of
my way!"
she cried.
"Princess
coming
through!"

In the shop, the very last game was just about to be wrapped.

Pansy pushed to the front of the queue.

"That game is mine!" she snapped.

"It's mine!
It's mine!"
yelled Princess Pansy.

"I got it!

Yippee!

Hooray!

I got the very last Super Stars game.

All I need to do now is play."

"Oh, dear," said Pansy, as she read the instructions to the game.
"It says, '*Two players or more to play,*' that really is a shame.

I'll have to find some children to play with. I don't have a choice."
So, Pansy stood on Neddy and **yelled** at the top of her voice.

"I've got the coolest game!" cried Pansy. "I know you want to play."

No one answered Princess Pansy. They just sighed and turned away.

There wasn't a single answer, not a whisper or a cry.
Only the sound of Neddy's hooves as he went
clip-clopping by.

"Hey, you," said a voice. "You jumped the queue. We don't think it's fair. There's nothing nice about a princess who doesn't want to share."

Pansy got off Neddy and he immediately clip-clopped home. Suddenly, Princess Pansy found herself alone.

The princess began to sob. She cried and bawled and moaned. "No one likes me," she wailed. "They think I'm spoiled," she groaned.

Pansy didn't want to be a royal princess any more. So, she took off her golden crown and threw it onto the floor.

"Don't cry," said two little girls, when they heard the terrible fuss.
"We are Katie and Cara," they said. "You can come and play with us."

Katie and Cara had paper crowns, old brooms and tatty dresses.
"We're riding our ponies," they said. "We're playing at princesses."

Princess Pansy put her crown on and found herself a broom. It was so much fun to laugh and play, she stayed all afternoon.

She rode through an enchanted kingdom that was really just pretend. "It's the best fun I've ever had," she said. "I don't want it to end."

"You're a really good princess," said the girls.
"We want to be like you!"
Princess Pansy whispered, sadly, "I wish that it was true."

She thought of
all her toys at
home and it made
her feel so sad.

"Maybe if I shared them," she
thought, "I wouldn't feel so bad."

"Come to my palace," said Pansy. "There's something I want to share."

"Wow!" cried Katie and Cara, when they saw all the toys that were there.

Princess Pansy invited friends to come and play every day. "I'll share my toys with YOU," she said and everyone cried, "Hurray!"

Princess Pansy had learned to share and when she was tucked up tight, she would happily dream of all her friends.

Goodnight, Princess Pansy, Goodnight.